Ma, Defender of the Sea

Written by Jen Campbell
Illustrated by Valentina Toro

Collins

Chapter 1

It started to rain as they hurried back inside the classroom after lunch. It was the last day of spring term and everyone was talking about where they were going for the school holidays. Lin said she was going to Greece for a week; Tariq said he was going to Portugal with his uncle. Amelia was telling anyone who would listen that she was going to Disneyland because, in case they'd forgotten, her mum had been given a big promotion at work.

"My sister and I have themed outfits," Amelia boasted. "I'll show you photos when we get back." She looked around the class and said insincerely: "It's such a shame you can't all come with us."

Max rolled his eyes and sat down at his desk. "Yes, such a shame," he whispered to Marceline. "She really does think she's the queen of the classroom."

"All hail, Queen Amelia," Marceline whispered back. "We are not worthy."

Most of the class were still gathered round Amelia, hanging on her every word. Marceline focused on unpacking her pencil case, not wanting to think about the upcoming holidays.

"I'll be thinking of you all when I watch the fireworks," said Amelia, "and I'll be thinking of you especially, Marceline," she called across the classroom. "How miserable to spend the holidays stuck inside a hospital!"

Marceline blushed. Trust Amelia to remind everyone that Marceline wasn't going away on holiday or relaxing at home.

Max sighed. "She's such a show-off."

Marceline changed the subject. "You'll have a fun holiday in Scotland, though. I'm always jealous of your caravan trips."

"It'll probably rain every day," he said. "And I'll be forced to play a million board games."

"Sounds great!" she grinned. "Send me a postcard of a Highland cow, please. It's tradition."

"Right, everyone. At your desks, please!" Miss Bhatt clattered through the classroom door, her hair damp from the rain and her glasses all steamed up. She nearly tripped over her own feet as she hurried to her desk, almost dropping the books she was carrying.

"Watch where you're going, Miss!"

"Yes, thank you, Jack." Miss Bhatt took a deep breath and waited for them to find their seats. "Now, I know it's the last day of term, but we still have work to do, and I need to talk to you about your holiday projects."

A collective groan sounded across the classroom.

Miss Bhatt tried not to look deflated. "Come on, everyone. Holiday projects don't ruin holidays; they are informative and entertaining!"

Most of the class looked unconvinced.

Miss Bhatt sighed. "Well, we're going to write some stories, and I'm sure that if you apply yourselves, you'll enjoy it. Over the next two weeks, I'm going to ask you to write a story based on a fairy tale." She indicated the pile of books she'd been carrying. "And I've brought some books with me for inspiration."

"But fairy tales are boring, Miss."

"They are not boring, Aisha." Miss Bhatt turned on the interactive whiteboard and a cartoon image of a princess in a ballgown and glass slippers appeared on the screen. "Who can tell me who this is?"

"Cinderella!"

"Quite so. She was a young woman with a horrible family, and she wasn't allowed to go to a royal ball. But a fairy godmother gave her a dress and glass slippers, and off she went. She had a great time, and even met the prince, but as she left the party in a rush at midnight, she left a glass slipper behind."

"The prince found the slipper and, having fallen in love with Cinderella, he searched all through the town to find her." Miss Bhatt clicked a button; the young woman in glass slippers disappeared, and in its place was a drawing of a girl talking to a golden fish. "And who is this?"

No one answered.

Miss Bhatt smiled. "This is Yeh-Shen. She is one of the world's oldest Cinderellas."

Amelia raised her hand. "She doesn't look like Cinderella, Miss Bhatt."

Miss Bhatt pointed at the whiteboard. "Ah, but you see, Cinderella is a fairy tale, and fairy tales have been around for thousands of years, and there are many different versions of the character of Cinderella."

Amelia looked as though she was going to disagree, so Miss Bhatt clicked the whiteboard again. "And what are these?"

Max raised his hand. "The Egyptian pyramids!"

"Quite right." She smiled at him. Max had won the class prize for his project on hieroglyphics last term.

Amelia frowned. "They're not in the Cinderella story either, Miss Bhatt."

"Ah, but they are!" Miss Bhatt threw her arms out wide which she always did when she was excited by something.

"You see, fairy tales are old stories created by communities. One person would make up a story and tell it to someone else. If they liked it, they would remember it and tell it to another person, and so on and so on, until one story could spread across many towns, sometimes countries, and even continents!"

Miss Bhatt pushed the books on her desk to one side and pulled herself up to sit on top of her desk, her legs swinging beneath her.

"Cinderella is one of our oldest fairy tales," she explained. "There's a version of Cinderella from Egypt which is over two thousand years old. It's about a woman called Rhodopis who loses her golden slipper. A pharaoh finds the slipper and goes on a quest to find and marry the person who owns it. Does that sound familiar?"

They all nodded.

"There are also versions of the Cinderella story from China from a thousand years ago," said Miss Bhatt. "In the Chinese story, the main character is called Yeh-Shen, and instead of a fairy godmother, she has a magical fish who makes her a beautiful gown to wear to a festival – a festival which her wicked stepmother has forbidden her to attend."

"And does she get to go to the festival, Miss Bhatt?"

"Yes, Lin, she does. You'll be pleased to hear that both Rhodopis and Yeh-Shen get to live happily ever after, much like the version of Cinderella that many of us know today."

Jack scoffed. "Happily ever afters aren't fun, though, Miss. I like scary stories."

Miss Bhatt's eyes twinkled. She clicked the whiteboard again and a drawing of a man with long wavy hair appeared. "Do you know who this is, Jack?"

He shook his head. "No, Miss."

"This is Charles Perrault. He wrote a version of Cinderella in French in the 17th century. Can you guess what happens in his version of the story, when the prince visits Cinderella's house at the end?"

Amelia put up her hand. "When the prince comes to Cinderella's house, the stepsisters try on the glass slipper but it doesn't fit them; it only fits Cinderella."

Miss Bhatt raised a finger. "Ah, but in Charles Perrault's version, the stepsisters are so desperate to fit inside the slipper, they get a knife, and do you know what they do with it? They cut off bits of their feet so they can fit inside the shoe!"

Cries of "ewww!" and "gross!" echoed across the room.

"Exactly!" said Miss Bhatt. "The prince was fooled by their actions at first but, as you can imagine, there was blood everywhere, and that's what gave them away." She paused. "While this is a story, we should also consider why these sisters felt they had to do something so brutal in order to find themselves a husband." She hopped down from the desk and started handing out books. "As you can see, fairy tales are not always straightforward happily ever afters. They are twisted tales, sometimes gory, often unpredictable, and they don't normally belong to one person, because they were told by word of mouth, by many people, hundreds of years ago."

Miss Bhatt beamed, seeing how interested they had all become. "These books that I'm passing out to you now are old collections of fairy tales. I would like you to spend the next hour reading some of these stories, and over the holidays I'd like you to write your own version of a fairy tale. Can you name some famous fairy tales aside from Cinderella that we can use as inspiration?"

"Snow White!"

"Sleeping Beauty!"

"Aladdin!"

"The Little Mermaid!"

"Little Red Riding Hood!"

"Very good," Miss Bhatt nodded. "I want you to pick a fairy tale and decide how you would like to retell it and put your own stamp on the story. Perhaps you could write it from a different character's point of view. You could change the setting or alter the ending. And yes, Jack, you are free to add scary elements if you want to do that, too; that's definitely in the spirit of old fairy tales!"

Chapter 2

When the bell went at the end of the day, everyone was talking about what fairy tales they were going to retell.

"I'm going to have a really horrible-looking villain in mine," Jack grinned. "They'll have an arm missing to make them properly scary."

Marceline flinched, pulling her jumper down over her hands.

"OK, everyone, have a revitalising break." Miss Bhatt had to raise her voice over the clamour. "Marceline, can I have a quick word before you go?"

As the last student left the classroom, Miss Bhatt came over to Marceline, holding out the red book she had been reading earlier. "It looked like you were enjoying this one," she smiled. "You can borrow it over the holidays, if you like."

Marceline's face lit up; she *had* been enjoying it. "Thanks!" She hugged the book to her chest. It was old and smelt of vanilla.

18

"Now, Marceline," said Miss Bhatt. "I received your mum's letter, and I wanted to say that if you can't manage to do your holiday project, that's absolutely fine ..." She trailed off, awkwardly.

Marceline was used to other people feeling awkward when they talked to her about her disability. This made her feel uncomfortable. She felt a strong urge to tell Miss Bhatt there was nothing to worry about. Sometimes she felt as though she spent so much time making sure other people felt OK, she forgot to ask herself the same question.

"I'd still like to write the story," said Marceline. "I'll only be in hospital for a few days. After that, I won't be able to use a pen for a few weeks, but I could try using voice recognition on my dad's laptop." Marceline had done that before, after a previous operation, speaking into a microphone. The laptop had written the words she was speaking. It hadn't guessed them all correctly, but Dad said that technology was improving all the time.

"Well, if you're able to do that, that would be lovely." Miss Bhatt walked her to the classroom door. "I hope your operation goes well. What number is this one?"

"Fifteen."

"Ouch!" Miss Bhatt patted her on the head. "It doesn't bear thinking about. You're a brave inspiration."

Marceline knew that Miss Bhatt was trying to be kind, so she smiled, but as she walked out of the school building to meet Max, the words "brave" and "inspiration" wriggled inside her stomach.

Marceline's mum had once explained to her that many non-disabled adults call disabled people "inspirational" and "brave" without really thinking about it, because they can't imagine living lives like theirs. To them, disabled people going about their everyday lives appears to be extraordinary when, really, they're just people doing people-like stuff. And while most people Marceline knew didn't have to have operations and physiotherapy and wear splints at night, she also knew there were lots of other people in the world who did have to do those things, and if everyone spoke about disability more openly, instead of calling her words like "special" or "inspirational", it would make her life a lot easier.

"Not that I don't think you're fabulous in other ways," her mum had said afterwards. "I mean, let's face it, the way you can eat ten pancakes in a row is definitely inspirational." And both Marceline and her mum had giggled about that for a long time.

Max and his dad were waiting for her at the school gates, and the three of them walked home along the seafront. The rain had stopped but you could still smell it, and as they made their way along the beach, Marceline looked out at the swelling tide.

Marceline's mum said she had chosen her name because it meant "defender of the sea". When Marceline had searched her name on the internet to check, lots of other meanings had popped up first, but when she'd scrolled all the way down, she'd finally found her mum's words. It was as though she'd dived right to the bottom of the internet to find them: "Marceline, defender of the sea"!

Marceline's name fitted her like a wetsuit. She adored the sea. She loved how it swallowed things whole and spat them back out again.

That afternoon, Marceline and Max collected shells that reminded them of broken stars, and as they left the sand and the pebbles to walk up to their road, Marceline glanced back at the water and wondered at all the stories swimming inside the sea's belly.

"See you soon, Marceline," said Max's dad, as she walked down the drive to her house. "We'll think of you on our travels."

"Thanks! And don't forget the postcard!" Marceline called back, waving them both goodbye.

Her mum was on a work call as Marceline came through the door. She waved to Marceline from her office and pointed into the kitchen where she'd left her a snack. Marceline took the snack up to her bedroom, where she saw her mum had also left a brand-new pair of pyjamas on her bed. Her parents always bought her a new pair of pyjamas as a treat before she went into hospital for an operation. While new pyjamas were a lovely thing, Marceline felt a bit weird about it, because whenever she wore those pyjamas afterwards, she was reminded of being in a hospital bed. However, these ones were particularly lovely; super soft and covered in starfish. She stroked them gently, deciding she would pack her hospital bag while her mum finished work.

25

Marceline was used to hospitals. She had been born with a type of Ectodermal Dysplasia, a disability that affected her body in lots of ways, including her hands, causing two things called syndactyly ("sin-dact-ily") and ectrodactyly ("ec-tro-dact-ily"). These two things meant that she'd been born with her fingers joined together, and some of her fingers missing, too. Marceline couldn't remember the very first operation she'd had, but she'd had many of them over the years, with surgeons separating her fingers and using metal pins, as well as skin grafts from her legs, to reshape her hands.

She looked down at them now. They didn't look like most people's hands; she had fewer fingers than most people, and the ones she did have were different shapes, covered in scars and different coloured pieces of skin. She moved them differently to other people, too, finding her own ways to hold a pen, tie her shoes, and help her mum chop vegetables in the kitchen. Sometimes people tried to make her feel bad about the way her hands looked, but they were her hands, and she was proud of them.

26

Marceline opened her empty backpack. She decided she would pack her new pyjamas, the red fairy tale book, some clothes for coming home, her toothbrush and toothpaste, and her headphones, too. She often found it painful to hold books open with her hands all bandaged up after an operation, though it was only her right hand they were operating on this time. Marceline liked listening to audiobooks, having stories whispered into her ears to distract her from all the hospital noises. She often used her mum's library app on her phone to download audiobooks for free. The library always amazed Marceline: so many stories out there, just waiting to be heard.

Her mum appeared in the doorway. "I've got a veggie pie in the fridge, but shall we go to the chip shop to get some chips to go with it?"

"Yes, please. Can we eat them out of the packet?"

"Is there any other way?" Her mum laughed. "Gravy or curry sauce?"

"Gravy, obviously."

"Obviously. Come on. Don't let me forget mushy peas for your dad; you know they're his favourite!"

Chapter 3

Waiting in the ward before the operation was the bit Marceline hated the most, because it all felt bigger inside her head. A nurse rubbed magic cream on the back of Marceline's left hand and stuck a clear plastic plaster over the top.

"It's numbing cream, so the anaesthetic injection doesn't hurt," Marceline told her dad, though of course they both knew that already. Saying facts out loud helped Marceline feel calmer. She pressed down on top of the plaster and giggled nervously; it felt strange.

"How's my water nymph?" Marceline's surgeon, Mrs Flood, strode into the ward with a smile. Marceline smiled back at her. Mrs Flood was one of the good doctors, someone who actually talked to Marceline, rather than just her parents – though Marceline always thought it was odd that surgeons were called "Mr" and "Mrs" instead of "Dr".

"I'm OK," she said, though that wasn't entirely true.

Mrs Flood raised a knowing eyebrow and opened her patient notes. "Well, I'm sure you'll be better than OK once we get this over and done with." She pulled a felt-tip pen out of her pocket and asked Marceline to hold out her right hand. She drew a dotted line on Marceline's skin between her thumb and index finger. "So, we're going to cut the skin back here, then once that's healed, you'll be able to stretch these two fingers wider, yes?"

"Yes." Marceline flexed her hand. Because she'd been born with her fingers joined together, and the doctors had separated them, sometimes the skin between her fingers grew back by mistake. This was called web creep, and occasionally the doctors had to remove it, so that Marceline could move her hands better. This was why Mrs Flood called Marceline her water nymph, like a mermaid – because lots of underwater creatures had webbed fingers and toes to help them swim. Marceline like this shared joke.

"Fabulous!" Mrs Flood snapped the patient file closed. "I'll see you in theatre, Marceline. Sweet dreams!"

When Marceline woke up from her operation, her vision was blurry, and her throat was dry, but she was only allowed to sip water slowly.

"It's like you're emerging from the sea, and back into the world," she heard Mrs Flood tell her parents. "Anaesthetic feels like that, doesn't it, Marceline? Like it sent you to sleep at the bottom of the ocean."

Marceline smiled weakly. It did feel like that, like she was floating somewhere strange. There were machines beeping near her head, and her right hand felt as though it was a fiery snowball.

Over the next few hours, she drifted in and out of sleep. Every so often she woke up and saw her mum trying not to look anxious, and she could hear her dad reading her stories from the red fairy tale book. Bits of the stories drifted into her brain as she slept. She dreamt of mermaids with webbed fingers, and she dreamt of the princess and the pea – imagining a young girl in an uncomfortable hospital bed that stretched up to the clouds.

After a few days, Marceline was allowed to go home. She still felt very tired, and her right hand was sore, but it always felt good to come home to her own bed.

"I want you to rest up," Mrs Flood had told her. "Listen to some books, eat some yummy food, and come back next week so we can change your bandages, OK?"

Marceline's hand throbbed dully, but when she got home she was thrilled to find a postcard sitting on their doormat with a picture of a furry orange cow. Max had remembered!

Marceline!

How are you? I hope your operation went well. I had to walk into town in the rain to find this postcard, and I don't think my socks will ever be dry again! BUT I was speaking to the guy in the shop, and he said there's an old local fairy tale about our caravan site, with a ghost and everything. How cool is that? Something to do with graveyards and a castle. He's lent me a book about it. I'm going to keep an eye out for the ghost ... actually, am I? Maybe I don't want to see a ghost ...

He handed her the small object, and Marceline held it in her left hand. "What's a dictaphone?"

He sat back down on the sofa. "Dictaphones are great things for collecting stories. You press this button here, then you speak into it, and it records what you're saying. So, if you have any story ideas while you're sitting in bed or on the sofa, you can speak them into this dictaphone and listen back to them later. No need for a pen or a computer at all."

Marceline smiled. "Thanks, Dad, that's really helpful."

"Just call me your fairy godfather."

She chuckled.

"So, do you think you'll use one of the fairy tales from the red book I was reading to you, for your fairy tale retelling?"

Marceline frowned. "I'm not sure, I haven't decided yet."

"Well, no rush, you've got plenty of time." Marceline's dad could sense that she wanted to say something more, so he nudged her leg gently. "What's up, little nymph?"

Marceline wasn't sure how to put her feelings into words, but she decided to try. "Well, when you were reading those fairy tales to me in the hospital, and when I've read other fairy tales before …" She trailed off and he looked at her encouragingly.

"I really like them, and they have lots of fun things like adventures and curses, and forests and mountains, but …" She paused, feeling the lump in her throat rising again. "None of the good guys look like me."

Her dad reached over and ruffled her hair. "Well, you are one of a kind, kiddo."

"No." Marceline shook her head quickly. "No, I'm not, Dad. I see other children with limb differences when we go to the hospital, and I see all kinds of disabled people out and about in the world – like our librarian, Miss Williams; and my swimming instructor, Mr Calder, and the woman who works in the café down the road; and loads of other people, too. But we're never shown as the good guys in these old fairy tales!"

Marceline's dad looked at her fierce expression, and he nodded slowly. "Sorry, little nymph. You're right."

She took a deep breath and said in a rush: "Most fairy tales have princesses who have smooth skin and no scars, and they don't have any visual differences, and everyone says they're beautiful." She paused. "Then the bad guys have burns and scars, and they look different, and people call them ugly and scary." The back of her eyes felt hot, and she blinked furiously. "And sometimes if those bad guys do good things, their bodies are magically cured as a reward."

Her dad smiled sadly. "It's all a bit boring, isn't it?"

Marceline nodded, looking down her at hands on top of the blanket. "It's boring, and unkind, and also not true." She winced at a sharp pain in her right hand. "People don't look different because they're bad or evil, and people aren't automatically good if they are not disabled, and no one gets a magic cure for good behaviour."

"Quite."

"And I know that stories are made up and not real," said Marceline, "but Miss Bhatt always told us that the best kinds of stories are the ones that still have some truth in them, even if they are magical."

Her dad pulled a tissue out of his pocket and gently wiped away Marceline's tears. "Well, it sounds like you already have some ideas for a story." Her dad smiled. "Turning some of these old fairy tales upside-down, to show that good and evil don't look a certain way. Hmm? What do you think about that?"

Chapter 4

So that's just what Marceline did.

Whenever she felt up to it, Marceline used the dictaphone her dad had given her to make up a fairy tale. She imagined a new version of The Little Mermaid, all about a water nymph with missing fingers, who didn't want to completely change her body like the Little Mermaid did, but who wanted to stay just as she was, having adventures in the sea. This water nymph made friends with other sea creatures whose bodies also looked different. They had a great time exploring the waves, and they worked hard to look after the sea by cleaning up plastic rubbish. Marceline grinned, remembering the meaning of her name: "Marceline: defender of the sea".

Marceline remembered what Miss Bhatt had said about it being traditional to tell fairy tales out loud, instead of writing them down. So, she practised speaking her story into the dictaphone until she was pleased with it, and on the last day of the holidays, when she was feeling a lot better, Marceline walked down to the beach with her mum, and they used the dictaphone to record the sound of the waves. They added that sound to the background of her story, so it sounded as though Marceline was speaking the words from the bottom of the sea.

Marceline was excited to share her story with the class — after all, stories were best when you shared them with other people.

"I bet Amelia won't like it," she said, as she walked to school with her mum. "She'll be too busy talking about her big holiday."

"Ah, I wouldn't worry about that," her mum said gently. "I was speaking to Amelia's mum the other day, and I don't think they had the best time. You know her parents are going through a divorce at the moment, don't you?"

"Yes," said Marceline. "But Amelia says that's not a big deal."

"Hmm." Her mum bent down and looked at Marceline. "I think we both know that sometimes we pretend to feel OK about things when we don't actually feel OK, don't we?"

Marceline thought about that and nodded.

"Not that feeling that way gives Amelia the right to be unkind to other people," her mum added. "But if it looks like she's showing off and pretending her life is wonderful, there may be a hidden reason for that." She gave Marceline a hug. "Anyway, have a good first day back, and let everyone hear your wonderful story, OK?"

Marceline blushed. "Thanks, Mum."

Marceline hurried into the school playground to find Max; she couldn't wait to hear all about his holiday and read his fairy tale retelling about the castle and the ghost. She couldn't wait to share her story with him, too.

When the time came, Marceline stood in front of the class holding the dictaphone above her head. She was nervous and excited. She pressed play, and the sound of the sea danced between the desks, followed by Marceline's voice declaring: "Once upon a time …"

Max gave her a thumbs-up. Marceline smiled. Her words seemed to fill every corner of the room. Everyone was listening to her underwater fairy tale – a fairy tale full of characters who were proud of their bodies, and all the stories that they held.

Diary entry, recorded on Marceline's dictaphone

"It's ten days after my operation. My hand is starting to itch, which means it's healing! I hope that when everyone in class sees the fairy-tale characters I've created, it makes them think carefully about the way characters' bodies are described in the stories we read."

Ideas for reading

Written by Gill Matthews
Primary Literacy Consultant

Reading objectives:
- check that the book makes sense to them, discussing their understanding and exploring the meaning of words in context
- draw inferences such as inferring characters' feelings, thoughts and motives from their actions, and justify inferences with evidence
- participate in discussions about books that are read to them and those they can read for themselves, building on their own and others' ideas and challenging views courteously

Spoken language objectives:
- use relevant strategies to build their vocabulary
- articulate and justify answers, arguments and opinions
- participate in discussions, presentations, performances, role play, improvisations and debates

Curriculum links: Relationships education – Caring friendships; Respectful relationships

Interest words: flinched, revitalising, awkward, inspiration, disabled

Build a context for reading
- Ask children to look at the front cover of the book. What do they think is happening?
- Read the back-cover blurb. Ask children how they think Marceline might be feeling.
- Focus on the references to fairy tales. Challenge children to name as many fairy tales as they can. Ask them to explain what they think a fairy tale is and what features it has.

Understand and apply reading strategies
- Read pages 2–9 aloud. Ask children what impression they get of Amelia and Miss Bhatt. Encourage them to support their responses with reasons and evidence from the text.